现代中国小小说 # Modern Chinese Mini–novels

U0132434

Published by:
The Commercial Press (U.S.) Ltd.
The Corporation, 2nd Floor
New York, NY 10013

Modern Chinese Mini-novels
Beginner Readings in Language and Culture

Author: Feng Mengqi
Editor: Edmond Hung

ISBN: 978 962 07 1955 4
Printed in Hong Kong

http://www.chinese4fun.net

Contents
目录

After studying one to two years of Chinese you have also gained the knowledge of quite a bit of vocabulary. You may be wondering whether there are any other ways for you to further improve your Chinese language proficiency? Although there are a lot of books in the market that are written for people who are studying Chinese it is not easy to find an interesting and easy to read book that matches up to one's level of proficiency. You may find the content and the choice of words for some books to be too difficult to handle. You may also find some books to be too easy and the content is too naive for high school students and adults. Seeing the demand for this kind of learning materials we have designed a series of reading materials, which are composed of vivid and interesting content, presented in a multi-facet format. We think this can help students who are learning Chinese to solve the above problem. Through our reading series you can improve your Chinese and at the same time you will learn a lot of Chinese culture.

Our series includes Chinese culture, social aspects of China, famous Chinese literary excerpts, pictorial symbols of China, famous Chinese heroes...and many other indispensable aspects of China for those who want to really understand Chinese culture. While enjoying the reading materials one can further one's knowledge of Chinese culture from different angles. The content of the series are contextualized according to the wordbase categorization of The content of the series are contextualized according to the word base categorization of HSK and GCS. We have selected our diction from the elementary, beginner, intermediate to advanced level of Chinese language learners. Our series is suitable for students at the pre-intermediate, intermediate to advanced level of Chinese and working people who are studying Chinese on their own.

The body of our series is composed of literary articles. The terms used in each article are illustrated with the romanised system called Hànyǔ pīnyīn for the ease in learning the pronunciation. Each article has an English translation with explanation of the vocabulary. Moreover there is related background knowledge in Expansion Reading. Interesting games are added to make it fun to learn. We aim at presenting a three-dimensional study experience of learning Chinese for our readers.

开店

Setting up shop

Pre-reading Questions

1. Do you like Chinese cuisine? What do you think is most appealing about Chinese cuisine?
2. Chinese cuisine is categorized into eight main types. Do you know what these eight types are?

---

❶ 两家饭店
Liǎng jiā fàndiàn

Wǒ jiā de pángbiān yǒu liǎng jiā xiǎo fàndiàn. Měi dào
我 家 的 旁边 有 两 家 小 饭店。 每 到

chīfàn de shíhou liǎng jiā fàndiàn li dōu zuòmǎn le kèrén
吃饭 的 时候, 两 家 饭店 里 都 坐满 了 客人。

Tīngshuō zhè liǎng jiā fàndiàn de shōurù hěn bù yīyàng
听说, 这 两 家 饭店 的 收入 很 不 一样。

Dì-èr jiā bǐ dì-yī jiā de shōurù gèng duō měi gè yuè
第二 家 比 第一 家 的 收入 更 多, 每 个 月

dōu duō jǐ qiān kuài qián Zhè shì wèishénme ne Wǒ fēicháng
都 多 几 千 块 钱。 这 是 为什么 呢? 我 非常

hàoqí
好奇。

Yī tiān wǒ zǒujìn dì-yī jiā fàndiàn Fúwù xiǎojiě
一天，我走进第一家饭店。服务小姐

gěi wǒ xiě wán cài zhīhòu yòu wèn Xiānsheng nǐ yào
给我写完菜之后，又问："先生，你要

jiā yī fèn xiǎochī ma Wǒmen de xiǎochī hěn shòu huānyíng
加一份小吃吗？我们的小吃很受欢迎

ne
呢！"

Wǒ shuō Hǎo ba nà jiù jiā yī fèn
我说："好吧，那就加一份。"

Wǒ kànkan zhōuwéi de rén tāmen dàduōshù dōu méiyǒu
我看看周围的人，他们大多数都没有

yào xiǎochī
要小吃。

Guò le yī tiān wǒ juédìng dào dì-èr jiā fàndiàn qù
过了一天，我决定到第二家饭店去

shìshi
试试。

A small restaurant

Xiě wán cài hòu
写完菜后，

fúwù xiǎojiě rèqíng de
服务小姐热情地

wèn Xiānsheng nǐ yào
问："先生，你要

jiā yī fèn xiǎochī háishi
加一份小吃，还是

jiā liǎng fèn ne Wǒ
加两份呢？"我

xiào le shuō Jiā yī
笑了，说："加一

fèn ba
份吧。"

又有一个客人进来。服务小姐问他：
"你要一份小吃，还是两份呢？"那位
顾客要了两份。

我一下子明白了。每位客人都加
小吃，一天就能卖出很多份。原来这家
饭店的收入就是这样多起来的！

❷ 最好喝的凉茶

在这个南方城市里，有不少大大小小
的凉茶店。

马路边，有一家不大的凉茶店，主人
是一位老奶奶。她经营这家店，已经
几十年了。有时候，我会买一杯凉茶，坐
下来跟老奶奶说说话。

有一次，我问她生意好不好。

老奶奶说："生意比从前差得多了。

Xiànzài yǒu nàme duō yǐnliào kěyǐ xuǎnzé, liángchá dōu
现在 有 那么 多 饮料 可以 选择，凉茶 都
kuàiyào bèi rén wàngjì le
快要 被 人 忘记 了。"

Wǒ shuō Duì a Nà wèishénme liángchádiàn háiyào
我 说："对 啊。那 为什么 凉茶店 还要
jiānchí xiaqu ne Tuìxiū huíjiā bùyòng zài xiǎng shēngyi
坚持 下去 呢？退休 回家，不用 再 想 生意
de hǎo yǔ huài bù hǎo ma
的 好与 坏，不好 吗？"

Lǎonǎinai xiào zhe shuō Suīrán liángchá de wèidao
老奶奶 笑着 说："虽然 凉茶 的 味道
méiyǒu biéde yǐnliào hǎo dànshì duì rén de shēntǐ yǒu
没有 别的 饮料 好，但是 对 人 的 身体 有
hǎochu hái néng zhìbìng Zǒngyǒu yī tiān rénmen huì chóngxīn
好处，还 能 治病。总有 一 天，人们 会 重新
àishàng hē liángchá de Yàoshi wǒmen bù jiānchí dàjiā
爱上 喝 凉茶 的。要是 我们 不 坚持，大家

A herbal tea shop

Herbal tea in a supermarket

yǐhòu jiù huì wàngjì liángchá zhè zhǒng dōngxi le
以后 就 会 忘记 凉茶 这 种 东西 了。"

Jiē zhe tā yòu gàosu wǒ zhǔ liángchá yào huā hěn duō
接着，她 又 告诉 我 煮 凉茶 要 花 很 多

gōngfu Měi yī zhǒng liángchá dōu néng zhìbìng Zuì kǔ de
功夫。每 一 种 凉茶 都 能 治病。最 苦 的

liángchá wǎngwǎng shì zuì hǎo de yǐnliào
凉茶，往往 是 最 好 的 饮料。

Tīng wán lǎonǎinai de huà wǒ zhōngyú míngbai wèishénme
听 完 老奶奶 的 话，我 终于 明白 为什么

nánfāng yǒu nàme duō liángchádiàn le
南方 有 那么 多 凉茶店 了。

Wǒ huì yīzhí zhīchí lǎonǎinai zhīchí liángchá
我 会 一直 支持 老奶奶，支持 凉茶。

Translation

❶ Two restaurants

Next to my home there were two small restaurants. During mealtimes, both restaurants were filled with customers.

I heard that the income earned by these two restaurants was very different. The second restaurant earned a lot more than the first one, as much as a few thousand dollars more every month. Why was that? I was very curious.

One day, I walked into the first restaurant. The waitress took my order, and then asked me: "Sir, do you want to add a side dish? Our side dishes are very popular!"

I said: "All right, I'll add one side dish then."

I looked at the people around me. Most of them did not order any side dishes.

The next day, I decided to try the second restaurant.

After writing down my order, the waitress asked me eagerly: "Sir, do you want to add one side dish, or two?" I smiled and said: "Let's add one."

Another customer came in. The waitress asked him: "Do you want one side dish, or two?" The customer ordered two side dishes.

Now I understood why. With every customer adding side dishes to their meals, many side dishes were sold in a day. So that was how this restaurant earned so much more income!

❷ The tastiest herbal tea

In a southern city, there were many big and small shops that sold herbal tea.

Beside the road was a small herbal tea shop that was owned by an old lady. She had been running this shop for quite a few decades. Sometimes, I would buy a cup of herbal tea, and then sit down and chat with the old lady.

Once I asked her if her business was good.

The old lady said: "Business is much poorer than before. Now with so many beverages to choose from, herbal tea is quickly being forgotten."

I said: "That's true. So why do you insist on running the herbal tea shop? You could retire and go home, and not worry about how the business is doing. Wouldn't that be great?"

The old lady smiled and said: "Although herbal tea is not as tasty as other beverages, it is good for the body, and can even cure illnesses. Someday people will love drinking herbal tea again. If we do not persist in carrying on, people will eventually forget all about herbal tea."

After that, she told me that preparing herbal tea took a lot of work. Every kind of herbal tea can cure illnesses. The most bitter herbal teas often make the best beverages.

After hearing what the old lady said, I finally realized why there were so many herbal tea shops in the south.

I will always support the old lady, and herbal tea.

Eating in China

A long time ago, the great educator Confucius said that "the people regard food as their heaven" (*minyishiweitian*; 民以食为天). Food has always occupied an important position in everyday life. That is why people in China have always placed great emphasis on eating and drinking.

In city streets of China, you can find all kinds of eating places, and there is no need to worry that you will not find anything to eat. There are big restaurants that are exquisitely and beautifully furnished, local and international fast food restaurants, no-frills ordinary eateries, as well as all kinds of speciality shops.

When people receive important guests, they often invite their guests to dine at a big restaurant. This is because the environment is more comfortable and cleaner, there is an abundant variety of dishes, and the quality of food is assured. Of course, the prices in such places will be more expensive.

People who live in cities lead a fast-paced life. To save time, many young people often eat at fast food restaurants. Nowadays many local fast food restaurants in China are learning from international fast food chains to implement standardized management, so that food quality and taste are assured. During the work week at noon or in the evening, these fast food restaurants are often packed with people.

However, ordinarily, the most frequented eating places are small simple eateries that are scattered up and down the streets. Whether it is congee, vermicelli, noodles, rice, or even stir-fried dishes, these eateries are authentic and cater to the local palate, so people never tire of eating at these places. With dishes for all three meals in a day, the food in these establishments is always able to satisfy people's needs.

Then there are all kinds of speciality shops, such as exotic foreign restaurants, and roadside food stalls that cater to the snacking urges of shoppers strolling on the streets. For any kind of eating place you can think of, you will be able to find it in China.

GAMES FOR FUN

Imagine you are treating some young Chinese people to a meal. Now look at the situations described below. Can you guess which eating place would make them the most happy?

1. Graduation cele
2. To have a chat
3. Ordinary breakfast
4. Everyday meal

A. Tea shop

B. Ordinary restaurant

C. Roadside stall

D. Fast food restaurant

Shēnchu bāngzhù de shǒu

伸出帮助的手

To lend a helping hand

Pre-reading Questions

1. Are you aware of what charitable organizations there are in China?

2. Have you ever received help from Chinese people?

Wǒ yào jiù māma
❶ 我 要 救 妈妈

Yī gè xiǎo nánhái zuò zài lùbiān měi jiàn rénmen
一 个 小 男 孩 坐 在 路边，每 见 人们

jīngguò jiù dàshēng wèn Xiānsheng nǐ yào cā píxié
经过，就 大声 问："先生，你 要 擦 皮鞋

ma
吗？"

Yī gè nánrén zuò xialai wèn Xiǎopéngyou tīng nǐ
一 个 男人 坐 下来，问："小朋友，听 你

shuōhuà nǐ bù shì běndìrén ba Nǐ niánjì zhème xiǎo
说话，你 不 是 本地人 吧。你 年纪 这么 小，

wèishénme bù qù shàngxué ne
为什么 不 去 上学 呢？"

Xiǎo nánhái yībiān cā xié yībiān shuō Jiālǐ
小 男孩 一边 擦 鞋，一边 说："家里
zhǐyǒu wǒ hé māma Māma bìng de hěn zhòng jiālǐ yòu
只有 我 和 妈妈。妈妈 病 得 很 重，家里 又
méi qián suǒyǐ wǒ zǒulù láidào zhèlǐ xiǎng duō zhuàn
没 钱，所以 我 走路 来到 这里，想 多 赚
diǎn qián gěi māma kànbìng Wǒ bù huì zuò biéde shìqing
点 钱 给 妈妈 看病。我 不 会 做 别的 事情，
zhǐhǎo cā píxié le Shūshu wǒ huì rènzhēn bǎ xiézi
只好 擦 皮鞋 了。叔叔，我 会 认真 把 鞋子
cā hǎo de Nǐ fàngxīn ba
擦 好 的！你 放心 吧！"

Zhège nánrén zhīdao xiǎo nánhái de jiāxiāng lí zhèlǐ
这个 男人 知道 小 男孩 的 家乡 离 这里
zhěngzhěng gōnglǐ Xiǎo nánhái yī gè rén zǒu zhème yuǎn
整整 600公里。小 男孩 一个 人 走 这么 远
de lù tā hěn gǎndòng
的 路，他 很 感动。

A roadside shoe polishing service

Tā gěi xiǎo nánhái liúxia
他 给 小 男孩 留下
le yuán Huídào jiālǐ
了 100元。回到 家里，
hái bǎ xiǎo nánhái de shìqing
还 把 小 男孩 的 事情
chuándào wǎngluò qù
传到 网络 去。

Hěnkuài hěn duō rén lái
很快，很 多 人 来
kàn xiǎo nánhái hái gěi tā
看 小 男孩，还 给 他
yīdiǎn qián Zhèngfǔ hé zhùrén
一点 钱。政府 和 助人

团体也知道了这件事，帮他把妈妈接到城市里看病。

后来，这个男人到医院去看小男孩和他的母亲，说："现在你不用擦皮鞋了。"

小男孩笑着说："是的！等妈妈的病好了，我要努力读书，将来也像叔叔一样帮助别人！"

❷ 站台上

早上，地铁站里站满了人。

一个老爷爷，带着一大包行李，看上去很着急。

他经常把头伸出站台去，看看车到了没有。看着看着，他一下子没注意脚下，就掉到站台下面。

车快要到了，可是站台有一米多

高，老爷爷很难爬上来。

有几个年轻人，赶紧过去抓住老爷爷的手，要把老爷爷拉上来。

有几个小学生，通知了地铁里的工作人员。

还有几位姑娘，帮忙看住老爷爷的行李。

年轻人们很快就把老爷爷拉了上来。

人们都走上前，问老爷爷有没有受伤。

老爷爷坐在椅子上，说："谢谢，谢谢！谢谢你们帮忙！"

不少人都说："你没事就好！以后要小心了！"

这时候，车到站了，年轻人帮老爷爷把行李拿上车。其它等车的人也都上车了。

Zhàntái   mǎshàng   ānjìng   xialai   Jiù   xiàng   cónglái   méiyǒu

站台 马上 安静 下来。就 像 从来 没有

fāshēng guo yìwài   yīyàng

发生 过 意外 一样。

Translation

❶ **I want to save my mother**

A boy was sitting by the road. Every time he saw a passerby, he would ask loudly: "Sir, do you want your leather shoes polished?"

A man sat down and asked him: "My little friend, you don't sound like a local. You are so young. Why aren't you in school?"

The boy polished the shoes as he spoke: "There is only me and my mother in my family. My mother is ill, and we have no money at home. That is why I walked all the way here to earn money to treat my mother. I do not have any other skills, and so I can only polish leather shoes. Uncle, I will be serious about polishing your shoes well! Do not worry!"

This man knew that the boy's hometown was a full 600 kilometers away from this place. He was touched that the boy walked such a long distance all by himself.

He gave the boy 100 yuan. When he got home, he even publicized the plight of the boy on the Internet.

Soon many people came to see the boy, and even gave him money. When the government and assistance groups learned about this, they helped him to send his mother to the city for treatment.

Later, this man went to the hospital to visit the boy and his mother, and said: "Now you no longer need to polish leather shoes."

The boy smiled and said: "That's right! When my mother has recovered, I must study hard, so that I can be like you and help other people in future!"

❷ On the platform

In the morning, the subway station was packed with people.

An old man was carrying a large piece of luggage, and he looked anxious.

He often stuck his head out of the platform to see if the train had arrived. While he was looking out for the train, he missed a step and fell into the space below the platform.

The train was approaching, but the platform was more than a meter tall, and the old man was having difficulty climbing back up.

A few young people quickly went over and grabbed the old man's hand to pull him up.

Some young students notified the subway staff.

And several ladies helped to watch over the old man's luggage.

The young people quickly pulled the old man back up. People expressed concern and asked if he was hurt.

The old man sat on a seat and said: "Thank you, thank you! Thank you for all your help!"

Many people said: "It's okay, so long as you are fine! Be careful next time!"

At that moment, the train arrived. The young people helped the old man to carry his luggage onto the train. The other passengers who were waiting also got on the train.

The platform immediately became quiet. It was as if no accident had ever happened.

It is a joy to help others

There is an old saying in China called *Zhuren wei kuaile zhi ben*(助人为快乐之本), which means it is a joy to help others. It is also a traditional virtue that is advocated by the Chinese people.

In today's Chinese society, although situations exist where people are selfish and only care about themselves, most people are still very willing to help others.

There are many niceties in everyday life that people are long accustomed to. Giving directions, relinquishing their seat and helping others in need are things that come naturally to people.

When major disasters strike, the altruistic spirit of the Chinese people is very evident. After a train derailed in an accident, hordes of people spontaneously went to hospitals to donate blood in support of relief efforts for the injured. After an earthquake struck, people were spontaneous in donating money and supplies to help the residents in the disaster zone to rebuild their homes. Such actions are a common occurrence.

Charitable organizations are also flourishing rapidly in China. Young people are increasingly keen to be social workers and volunteers. During their free time from studies or work, they will join various activities organized by charitable organizations, and contribute money and effort to help people within the country more needy than themselves. They are not afraid of hard work. Some of them go to remote mountainous areas to support local education efforts, some visit destitute old folks, while some take part in counseling programs for wayward youths.

More and more people in China believe that helping others will truly bring joy to their own life. The saying *Zhuren wei kuaile zhi ben* really makes sense.

怎样买东西

How to buy things

Pre-reading Questions

1. Whenever you encounter a sales promotion at a store, around how many items would you buy?

2. 2. Have you ever come across stores that offer really good value? What qualities do they have in common?

Mǎi píxié

❶ 买皮鞋

Chūn Jié kuài dào le Lǎo Wáng yào mǎi yī shuāng xīn píxié
春节 快 到 了，老 王 要 买 一 双 新 皮鞋。

Zài yī jiā shāngdiàn li Lǎo Wáng kàndào le yī shuāng
在 一 家 商店 里，老 王 看到 了 一 双

píxié tā hěn xǐhuan
皮鞋，他 很 喜欢。

Shòuhuòyuán rèqíng de shuō Zhè shuāng píxié hěn
售货员 热情 地 说："这 双 皮鞋 很

hǎo yuán xiànzài zhǐyào yuán jiù mǎidào piányi
好，880 元，现在 只要 440 元 就 买到，便宜

le yībàn
了 一半。"

老王一听"440"，心里想："四百四，就像'死白死'，真不好听！"

所以，他看也没看售货员，就走了。

在另外一家商店，老王又看到了一双同样的皮鞋。皮鞋上有个牌子，写着"一元变两元"。

老王很奇怪。

旁边的售货员笑着说："在我们店里买东西，一元能当两元用！你不用500元，就能买到这双880元的皮鞋了！"

老王听到皮鞋便宜了那么多，他立刻买下，拿着皮鞋高兴地走了。

Tag line for a promotional offer in a store

❷ 超市 真的 便宜 吗

小李 的 家 旁边，有 一 家 大 超市。

在 春节 前，超市 举行 了 一 次 优惠
活动。

小李 很 早 就 过去 了，希望 能 买到
便宜 的 东西。

超市 里 挂 满 了 广告。这 张 写 着 "买
一 送 一"，那 张 写 着 "买 满 100 元 送 10
元 优惠券"。

小李 很 高兴，今天 买 东西 真 便宜 啊！

到 了 超市服务台，工作人员 说："先生，
你 要 的 东西 一共 199 元。你 要 多 买 一点
东西，才 可以 有 20 元 优惠券 呢！"

小李 听 了，只好 回去 买 了 一 瓶 10 元
的 牛奶。拿 着 20 元 优惠券，小李 又 买 了
几 斤 水果，还 补 了 5 元。

18

第二天，小李的
Dì-èr tiān Xiǎo Lǐ de

妈妈 来到 他 家。看到
māma láidào tā jiā Kàndào

牛奶，说："我 也 买
niúnǎi shuō Wǒ yě mǎi

了 这 种 牛奶。才 8
le zhè zhǒng niúnǎi Cái

元，真 便宜。"
yuán zhēn piányi

小李 说："什么？
Xiǎo Lǐ shuō Shénme

我 昨天 买 的 是 10 元
Wǒ zuótiān mǎi de shì yuán

啊！"
a

Tag line for a special offer in a supermarket

Translation

❶ Buying leather shoes

The Spring Festival was almost here. Lao Wang wanted to buy a new pair of leather shoes.

In one of the stores, Lao Wang saw a pair of leather shoes that he liked.

The salesperson said eagerly: "This is an excellent pair of shoes. The price was 880 yuan, but now you can buy it for just 440 yuan, which is cheaper by half."

When Lao Wang heard "440", he thought: "Four hundred and forty sounds like 'to die in vain'. It sounds really awful!"

And so, without even so much as looking at the salesperson, he left.

In another store, Lao Wang saw a similar pair of leather shoes. On the shoes was a sign that read: "One yuan becomes two."

Lao Wang was curious.

The salesperson beside him said with a smile: "When you buy things in our store, one yuan can be used as two yuan! You need only spend less than 500 yuan to buy this pair of leather shoes worth 880 yuan!"

When Lao Wang heard that the shoes were so much cheaper, he bought them at once, and happily left the store with new leather shoes.

❷ Is the supermarket really cheaper

Next to Xiao Li's home was a large supermarket.

Prior to the Spring Festival, the supermarket held a promotional event.

Xiao Li went there early, as he hoped to buy things cheaply.

In the supermarket, there were many advertisements. One said "buy one get one free," while another said "get a 10-yuan voucher for every 100 yuan worth of items purchased."

Xiao Li was happy. It was so cheap to buy things that day!

At the supermarket's service counter, the staff said: "Sir, the items you want cost a total of 199 yuan. You only need to buy a bit more to get a 20-yuan voucher!"

When Xiao Li heard that, he went back to get a 10-yuan bottle of milk. With the 20-yuan voucher, Xiao Li bought a few catties of fruit, but he also had to top up another 5 yuan.

The next day, Xiao Li's mother came to his place. On seeing the milk, she said: "I also bought milk like this. It was only 8 yuan. That was really cheap."

Xiao Li said: "What? I bought this yesterday for 10 yuan!"

Mad about shopping

People the world over love shopping, and the Chinese people are no exception.

In China, on New Year's Day and other festivals, or during the change of seasons, many retailers offer crazy discounts and sales promotions. Shopping for things at these times gives more value for money than usual.

For instance, you can see many stores with signs that say "prices from 30 percent," or even "as low as 10 percent" that brighten the eyes of people who love shopping, and rush in to take their pick. There are some stores that use gimmicks such as "buy 100 yuan worth of items and get 50 yuan free" or even "buy 100 yuan worth of items and get 80 yuan free" to attract customers. People feel that this is equivalent to paying just 50 percent or even 20 percent of the price of the goods, and so do not hesitate to buy more. Especially during National Day, or the Golden Week during the Spring Festival, people have longer holidays, and go to the stores to shop. Some large department stores can earn in just a few days several hundred million yuan in sales.

Nowadays more and more young people in China like to shop online, and so online stores also carry out sales activities from time to time, for instance on their website anniversary or store celebrations. On China's largest online shopping platform, Taobao.com, the daily transaction volume in 2010 reached 900 million yuan.

However, in a time when people are mad about shopping, whether the discounts that retailers offer are really value for money, or whether the so-called sales promotions are really beneficial to the consumer, should still be evaluated with a rational mind and carefully considered. After all, the Chinese

Tag line for a closing-down clearance sale

people like to say *maide buru maide jing* (买的不如卖的精), which means the buyer is not as wise as the seller.

GAMES FOR FUN

Imagine you are in China, and today a large shopping mall has a promotional event with the promotions listed below. If you want to buy a few shirts that cost around 150 yuan each, a pair of shoes that cost 499 yuan, and daily necessities worth around 150 yuan, but your total expenditure cannot exceed 1,200 yuan, what would you buy to get the most value for your money?

买满200送100现金券

(Buy 200 yuan worth of items and get a 100-yuan cash voucher free.)

买一件八折，两件七折，三件六折

(Buy one piece at 80 percent of the original price, two pieces at 70 percent of the original price, three pieces at 60 percent of the original price.)

买满300元可以免费停车一小时，不设上限

(Buy 300 yuan worth of items and get one hour parking free, no limit to the number of hours of parking redeemable.)

Answer for reference:

1. First buy three shirts. You need to pay a total of 450 yuan, and you will get 200 yuan worth of cash vouchers;
2. Use the cash vouchers worth 200 yuan to buy the shoes. You need to pay 299 yuan, and you will then get a 100-yuan cash voucher;
3. Use the 100-yuan cash voucher to buy daily necessities. You need to pay another 50 yuan;
4. The final amount spent is 799 yuan, which will get you two hours of free parking.

Gōngzuò de wèntí

工作的问题

Problems at work

Pre-reading Questions

1. What line of work would you like to be in? Why?

2. When a piece of work requires you to work overtime to finish , do you think that it is more important to finish the work, or is it more important to have your personal time and space?

---

❶ Nǎge gèng zhòngyào
哪个 更 重要

Tā liánxù sān tiān dōu zài gōngsī gōngzuò méiyǒu
他 连续 三 天 都 在 公司 工作， 没有

huíjiā
回家。

Zhè xiàng gōngzuò hěn zhòngyào lǎobǎn shuō yīdìng yào zài
这 项 工作 很 重要， 老板 说 一定 要 在

Xīngqīwǔ zhīqián wánchéng Suǒyǐ dàjiā dōu zài gǎn tiāntiān
星期五 之前 完成。 所以 大家 都 在 赶， 天天

jiābān
加班。

Māma dǎdiànhuà lái shuō Érzi nǐ zěnme tiāntiān
妈妈 打电话 来 说："儿子， 你 怎么 天天

要加班啊！这样的工作别做了！"

他说："妈妈，这份工作的工资很好呢！赚的钱多，当然会忙一点。"

好不容易忙完工作，他就生病了。

妈妈的心很痛，说："儿子，身体重要啊！工作可以选另一份，但健康如果没有了，受苦的是自己呀！"

听完妈妈的话，他开始认真地想：到底是工作重要，还是身体重要呢？不忙的工作，赚钱不多，很难买房子，更别说更好的生活了；赚钱多的工作，往往很忙，忙得常常没有时间跟家里人一起吃饭。这真是一个难题啊！

你的选择会是什么呢？

❷ 奇怪的考试题

一家大公司里，六个年轻人正在认真地在做考试的题目。

这些年轻人都通过了很多次考验，这次考试是最后一场。

通过考试的人，就可以进入这家世界有名的大公司工作。

考试的题目一共有20道。负责考试的人说："请先看一遍考试的要求，然后在10分钟之内完成。"

大家看到那么多题目，只有10分钟去做，都很紧张。多数人拿起了题目就马上开始做，心里不断地想怎样才可以多做几道题。

10分钟后，大家都停下来。有的人说："我才做了6道题目，真难啊！"

有的人说：“我比你好，我做了10道题！不知道谁能做完呢？”

只有一个年轻人奇怪地说：“为什么要做那么多题目呢？考试要求上说，只需要做最后的两题啊！”

“啊！”一下子，大家都安静了下来。

最后，只有一个人通过了考试。那就是这位只做了两道题目的年轻人。

Recruitment advertisement

Translation

❶ Which is more important

A man had been working in his office for three consecutive days without going home.

His work was important, and the boss had said that it must be finished by Friday. Everyone was rushing and working overtime every day.

His mother phoned him and said: "Son, why do you need to work overtime every day! Stop doing this kind of work!"

He said: "Mother, the salary for this job is good! Since it pays more, I will naturally have to work a bit more."

After rushing to finish the work with great difficulty, he fell ill.

His mother said kindly: "Son, take care of your health! You can always choose another job, but if you lose your health, it is you who will suffer!"

After hearing his mother's words, he started to think hard: Is work more important, or is health more important? A job that is not as demanding will not pay well, making it difficult to buy a house, not to mention have a better life; a job that pays more is often more demanding, making one so busy that often there is no time to eat together with the family. This is such a difficult problem!

What would your choice be?

❷ An unusual test

In a large company, six young people were working hard on some test questions.

These young people had been through many tests, and this would be their final round.

Those who passed the test would be able to work in this large world-renowned company.

There were 20 test questions in total. The examiner said:

"Please read the test requirements, and then finish the test within 10 minutes."

When everyone saw there were so many questions to be done in only 10 minutes, they all became tense. Many people started doing the questions the moment they received them, and in their mind they were constantly thinking how to do as many questions as possible.

Ten minutes later, everyone had stopped. Some said: "I only did six questions. It was really difficult!"

Others said: "I did better than you. I did ten questions! I wonder if anyone managed to finish?"

Only one young man said puzzlingly: "Why was there a need to do so many questions? The test requirements said we only needed to do the last two questions!"

"What?" Everyone was suddenly quiet.

In the end, only one person passed the test. It was the young man who did only two questions.

Expansion Reading

Work choices

Of the young people in China today, most are faced with a dilemma between earning income and their personal health or life.

A high income often implies intensive and stressful work. Every day one has to face many complex tasks, and working overtime at night or on weekends is commonplace. There was one such young lady with a master's degree who worked at an accountancy firm. After working overtime nonstop for a week, she fell ill and suddenly died. This led to much criticism from the entire society about such intensive work.

In contrast, work that is relatively leisurely and less stressful often means a lower income. In today's China, the cost of living in cities is getting higher and higher. If one's income is low, life may be filled with anxiety. Do you want to stay in a larger house? Or to go traveling from time to time? Both are impossible to achieve!

Most young people who have just graduated from school and started work want to be successful in their career. During this process, they often need to sacrifice their personal leisure time and space, and even their own health, in exchange for a high salary and a good position. However, for most people, even before they can get any of the rewards that they have hoped for, they are already defeated by setbacks, and have to accept reality gradually resigning themselves to a mediocre existence. As for those young people who do manage to gain good rewards, they often have to pay an irrevocable price where their health is concerned.

In spite of this, every year droves of young people join the ranks of this army of people doing intensive work.

Are you also like many young Chinese people who face a choice between work and personal life? What would you do?

GAMES FOR FUN

Look at the people in the pictures below. Can you guess what their respective occupations are?

(1) 衬衫西裤的白领人士 (2) 孙悟空 (3) 咨客 (4) 道士

A. Actor
B. Priest
C. Store receptionist
D. Attendant at a restaurant to welcome and seat customers
E. Attendant at a restaurant
F. Employee at a trading firm

Chéngshì li de àiqíng

城市里的爱情

Romance in the city

Pre-reading Questions

1. In your country, what kind of attitude do most young people have towards romance?
2. What would you need to sort out before choosing to get married?

Xiāngpèi bù xiāngpèi

❶ 相配 不 相配

Xiǎo Wáng láizì nóngcūn Kǎo shàng dàxué zhīhòu tā liú
小 王 来自 农村。考 上 大学 之后，他 留

zài chéngshì li nǔlì gōngzuò
在 城市 里 努力 工作。

Xiǎo Zhāng chūshēng zài chéngshì Fùmǔ zhǐyǒu tā yī gè
小 张 出生 在 城市。父母 只有 她 一 个

háizi suǒyǐ duì tā hěn hǎo
孩子，所以 对 她 很 好。

Zài yī cì gōngzuò zhōng Xiǎo Wáng rènshi le Xiǎo Zhāng
在 一 次 工作 中，小 王 认识 了 小 张。

Xiǎo Wáng xǐhuan Xiǎo Zhāng piàoliang kě'ài Xiǎo Zhāng bèi Xiǎo Wáng
小 王 喜欢 小 张 漂亮 可爱，小 张 被 小 王

的 经历 感动。 两 个 人 走 在 一 起， 感情 很
好。

后来， 在 准备 结婚 的 时候， 事情 有 了
变化。

小 王 要 和 农村 的 父母 一起 住。 他
说："他们 把 我 养大， 结婚 之后 要 让 他们
在 城市 里 过上 好 生活。"

小 张 说："有 老人， 两 个 人 就 没有
自由 了。 我 不 愿意 跟 老人 一起 住。"

小 王 认为 只要 领 了 结婚证 就 行，
把 钱 省 下来 可以 在 家乡 请 亲人 朋友们
吃饭。

小 张 说："我 一直 都 希望 能 有 一 个
很 好 的 婚礼！"

小 王 的 妈妈 送给 小 张 一 个 金 戒指。
小 王 认为 有 一 个 金 戒指 就 够 了。

小张 说："现在 谁 还 喜欢 金 戒指 呢？
大家 都 有 钻石 戒指 的 呀！"
就 这样，他们 每 天 为 各种 小事 争 个
不停。不久，他们 分开 了。
最后，小 王 结婚 了，他 的 太太 来自
农村。小 张 也 结婚 了，丈夫 和 她 一样，
是 在 城市 里 长大 的 孩子。
中国人 常 说，两 个 人 要 相配，才能
在 一起 生活。也许，相配 的 意思，就 有 了
城市 和 农村 的 区别。

The "double happiness" character displayed
during Chinese weddings

A gold ring worn when one gets married

❷ 让 我们 一起 努力

他们 结婚 了。

他们 没有 自己 的 房子。新 的 房子 是 租
来 的 一 个 小 房间，离 市 中心 很 远。

他 很 想 换 一 间 大 房子，让 太太 住
得 舒服 一点。所以 结婚 之后，他 很 努力 地
工作。

不久，她 发现 他 总是 很 晚 才 回家，很
不 开心。

那 天 晚上，他 又 工作 到 很 晚 才
回家。她 很 生气，问："你 知道 我 天天 都
在 等 你 回家 吗？"

他 也 生气 了："我 天天 努力 工作，才
会 这么 晚！我 都 是 为了 让 你 能 住上 大
一点 的 房子！"

说 完，他 就 坐 在 椅子上 没有 再 说话。

看到 他 不再 说话，她 找 出 一 张 纸，

在 上面 写："别 再 生气 了 好 吗？以后

我们 一起 努力 工作！"然后，再 画 上 一 个

笑脸。

看到 这 句 话，他 看 着 她，笑 了。

那天 晚上 之后，他 工作 还是 很 忙，

但 总会 早 一点 回家。她 白天 也 很 忙，但

下班 以后，就 会 做 好 饭，等 他 回来 一起

吃。

一 年 之后，他们 搬家 了。房子 还是 租

的，但 离 市 中心 已经 很 近 了。

A house that the common people live in

Translation

❶ Compatible or not

Xiao Wang came from the countryside. After he graduated from university, he remained in the city and worked hard in his job.

Xiao Zhang was born in the city. She was her parents' only child, and so they doted on her.

During one job, Xiao Wang met Xiao Zhang and they got to know one another. Xiao Wang liked Xiao Zhang for being attractive and adorable, while Xiao Zhang was touched by Xiao Wang's experience. The two got together, and their relationship was good.

Later, as they prepared to get married, things changed.

Xiao Wang wanted to live together with his parents from the countryside. He said: "They toiled to raise me, so after we get married, I want them to come to the city and have a good life."

Xiao Zhang said: "With old people around, the two of us will not have any freedom. I am not willing to live with old people."

Xiao Wang thought it would be enough to just obtain a marriage certificate, and use the money saved to treat his relatives and friends in the village to a meal.

Xiao Zhang said: "I have always hoped to wear a wedding gown, and have a proper wedding!"

Xiao Wang's mother gave Xiao Zhang a gold ring. Xiao Wang thought just one gold ring would be enough.

Xiao Zhang said: "Who likes gold rings nowadays? Everyone has a diamond ring!"

And so, they quarreled every day over all kinds of minor issues. Not long after this, they broke up.

In the end, Xiao Wang got married. His wife came from the countryside. Xiao Zhang also got married. Her husband, like her, was someone who grew up in the city.

The Chinese people often say that two people must be compatible in order to live together. Perhaps the meaning of being "compatible" includes the distinction between the city and the countryside.

❷ Let us work hard together

A couple got married.

They did not own their own house. They lived in a small rented apartment that was far from the city center.

He wanted to change to a bigger place, so that his wife could live more comfortably. And so, after their marriage, he worked very hard.

Soon after, she found that he was always getting home late, and she was not happy.

One night, he got home late from work again. She was angry, and asked him: "Do you know that every day I wait for you to return home?"

He also got angry: "I work hard every day. That is why I am home late! I am doing all this so that you can live in a bigger place!" After saying this, he sat down on a chair and did not say another word.

Seeing that he had gone silent, she took a piece of paper and wrote: "Don't be angry anymore, okay? Let us work hard together from now on!" Then she drew a smiley face.

Upon seeing these words, he looked at her and smiled.

After that night, although he was still busy with work, he always managed to come home a little earlier. She was also busy during the day, but after she got off work, she would prepare a good dinner, and wait for him to come home so they could eat together.

A year later, they moved to another house. The new place was still rented, but it was much nearer to the city centre.

Modern love stories

In Chinese cities, there are modern love stories like these that are playing out every day:

A couple had been dating since the start of university, and their relationship was good. Before they graduated, both had decided on different plans for their future and wanted to go to different cities, so they broke up in the end;

A boy from the countryside who was diligent in his studies, whom the Chinese people refer to as a 凤凰男 (*fenghuangnan*; "phoenix man"), met a girl who grew up in the city, whom the Chinese people refer to as a 孔雀女 (*kongquenu*; "peacock woman"). Both were attracted to each other and they started a relationship. However, because the two grew up in vastly different environments, they also broke up in the end;

There was a married couple who had a good relationship. Nevertheless, due to the involvement of a third party, or poor management of the relationship between the wife and the mother-in-law, they quarreled every day and still broke up in the end.

These scenarios are getting more and more common in today's China. Young people place less emphasis on marriage than the older generation. The older folks can never understand this: Among the young people of today, how much do they really respect love and marriage commitments?

Of course, there are also couples who love each other and grow old together. The truth is, such couples often have similar world views and values, can understand each other and are willing to make sacrifices for each other. Today, there are more and more only children who receive all the pampering from the entire family, and people who understand sharing and sacrifice are becoming less and less common.

Wǒmen hé tāmen

我们和他们

Us and them

Pre-reading Questions

I. In the city where you live, are there many people who come from other countries or regions? Where are the different places that they come from?

2. Do you have friends from other countries or regions? During your interaction with them, do you encounter any problems in communication?

Wǒmen dōu yīyàng
❶ 我们 都 一样

Zhè tiān yī gè shāngdiàn mén qián liǎng gè rén zài
这 天 ，一 个 商店 门 前 ，两 个 人 在

zhēng zhe shénme Pángbiān wéi le hěn duō rén
争 着 什么 。旁边 围 了 很 多 人 。

Yī gè nánrén yòng wàidì kǒuyīn dàshēng shuō Wǒ
一 个 男人 用 外地 口音 ，大声 说 ："我

méiyǒu tōu dōngxi
没有 偷 东西 ！"

Yī gè diànyuán shuō Rúguǒ nǐ méiyǒu tōu
一 个 店员 说 ："如果 你 没有 偷 ，

为什么你拿着这瓶牛奶就走？"

外地男人说："我只是要拿回去放牛奶的地方，你还没看清楚，为什么说我偷东西呢？"

店员说："你们这些外地人，就喜欢偷东西！我们已经捉住好几个小偷，都是外地人！"

可能因为生气，外地男人脸都红了。

他不断地说："我是外地人，可是我不是小偷……"

这时，一个女孩子从一群人中走出来，对店员说："他不是小偷！我看到那瓶牛奶早就被人放在这里了！"

店员很生气，对女孩子说："你为什么要帮这个外地人呢？"

女孩子说："这是事实！不能因为他

是外地人，就说他偷东西。"

最后，店员不能证明男人要偷
东西，只好放走他。

外地男人非常感谢女孩。女孩笑了笑
说："我只是说出了我看到的情况。我
相信，外地人也有很多好人啊！"

A crowded supermarket

❷ 小饭店，大家庭

在她家楼下，有一家小饭店。她不想做饭的时候，就会到那里吃饭。

小饭店里由一对夫妇经营。不论多忙，他们对客人的态度都很好，经常笑着。

这天，天气很冷。她感冒了，但为了完成工作，还是加班到很晚。到了家的楼下，她看到小饭店还开着门，店里有两三个客人，温暖的灯光照亮店外的路。

她走进去，说："老板，来一碗面吧。"

太太关心地问："你感冒了？怎么还工作到这么晚啊！要小心身体呢！"

她笑了笑，说："没办法，工作太忙了。"

这时 丈夫 拿 过来 一 碗 面，说："赶紧
吃 吧，我 多 放 了 姜，你 多 喝 点 汤，回去
睡觉 不 会 很 难受 了。"

她 喝 了 汤，不仅 身体 暖和 了，心 也
暖和 起来。

这时候，一 个 客人 说："老板，今天 真
冷，你 也 早点 回家 休息 吧。"其它 客人 都
点头。

老板 笑 着 说："好 啊，等 你们 吃 完，
我们 收拾 好 就 回家。你们 工作 忙，晚上
也 要 吃点 东西 才 好 睡觉。"

说 笑 了 一会儿，

大家 就 各自 回家。

不久，小店 关上

了 门，街上 也 安静

了 下来。

A small roadside restaurant

Translation

❶ We are all the same

One day, two people were arguing in front of the entrance to a store. Many people gathered around.

A man said loudly in a foreign accent: "I did not steal anything!"

A store assistant said: "If you did not steal anything, why are you walking off with this bottle of milk?"

The foreign man said: "I only wanted to put the milk back in its place. You did not see this clearly, why do you say I am stealing things?"

The store assistant said: "Foreigners like you tend to steal things! We have already caught quite a few thieves, and they are all foreigners!"

The face of the foreign man was red, probably from anger. He kept saying: "I am a foreigner, but I am not a thief."

A girl squeezed out from the crowd, and said to the store assistant: "He is not a thief! I saw that this bottle of milk was misplaced by someone else!"

The store assistant was angry, and said to the girl: "Why are you helping this foreigner?"

The girl said: "This is the truth! You cannot say he is stealing things just because he is a foreigner."

In the end, the store assistant could not prove that the man was stealing, and so had to let him go.

The foreign man was grateful to the girl. The girl smiled and said: "I only said what I saw. I believe there are many foreigners who are good people too!"

❷ Small restaurant, big family

There was a small restaurant downstairs from a woman's home. Whenever she did not feel like cooking, she would eat there.

The small restaurant was run by a couple. No matter how busy they were, they always treated their customers with hospitality, and smiled often.

One day, the weather was cold. The woman had caught a cold, but because she had to finish some work, she continued to work overtime until it was very late. When she reached her home, she saw that the small restaurant was still open. In the restaurant were two or three customers, and its warm lights lit up the road outside.

She walked in and said: "Boss, one bowl of noodles please."

The lady boss asked her with concern: "Have you caught a cold? Why are you still working so late! Please take care of your health!"

She smiled and said: "I have no choice, it's been too busy at work."

The husband brought a bowl of noodles and said: "Please eat this quickly, I have put in extra ginger. Drink more soup, and you will feel better when you go home and sleep."

She drank the soup. Not only did it warm her body, it warmed her heart as well.

Then a customer said: "Boss, it's cold today. You go home early and rest too." The other customers nodded.

The boss said with a smile: "All right. When you have finished, we will pack up and go home. You work hard, and also need to eat something to have a good night's sleep."

After some chatting, everyone went back to their own homes.

Soon after, the small shop closed its doors, and the street went quiet.

How Chinese people get along with others

Chinese people are often taught that "the friendship of gentlemen should be pure like water" (*junzizhijiaodanrushui*, 君子之交淡如水), that is they should not come into close contact with other people too easily, and they should maintain a certain distance.

When it comes to strangers, Chinese people have always adopted a certain cautious mentality to avoid getting themselves hurt. This belief in self-protection has led many to think that Chinese people are indifferent. Actually, to the Chinese people, it is important to first protect oneself before one can do anything else. They do not think that this is a bad thing.

However, when it comes to relatives, friends or neighbors, Chinese people are a lot more passionate. They view these people as their "own people", and often have the instinct to protect them. When their "own people" encounter any problem, they will eagerly and actively help to solve the problem as quickly as possible. They usually spend time with their "own people", orarrange get-togethers. Even if it is just running into one another on the street, or calling each other casually on the phone, they can chat for half a day.

Today, in many large cities in China, such as Beijing, Shanghai and Guangzhou, the migrant population is increasing rapidly. These people who come from all across the country and settle in large cities find it easier to empathize with one another. However, it is not easy for foreigners and locals to get along. The increase in foreigners leads to fewer resources and work opportunities for the locals, whose way of life is also disrupted. This is why they often have a prejudice that ostracizes foreigners. The governments of many large cities are working hard to change this, in the hope of reducing the conflict between the two. Because it is only when people can get along compatibly that a harmonious society can be achieved.

Gèzhǒng-gèyàng de sījī

各种各样的司机

All kinds of drivers

Pre-reading Questions

1. In your home city, whenever there is a traffic jam, what do people like to do to pass time?

2. In your country, what kind of penalties do drunk drivers face?

---

❶ 两个司机
Liǎng gè sījī

Wǒ zhù zài yī gè dà chéngshì li　　Měi tiān zǎoshang qù
我 住 在 一 个 大 城 市 里。每 天 早 上 去

shàngbān de rén hěn duō　　chē yě hěn duō
上班 的 人 很 多，车 也 很 多。

Yǒu yī tiān　　wǒ qǐchuáng wǎn le　　Wǒ gǎnjǐn zuòshàng
有 一 天，我 起 床 晚 了。我 赶 紧 坐 上

chūzūchē　　xīwàng kuàidiǎn huídào gōngsī
出租车，希 望 快 点 回 到 公 司。

Mǎlùshang qìchē hěn duō　　chūzūchē zǒu de hěn màn
马路上，汽 车 很 多，出 租 车 走 得 很 慢。

Wǒ shuō　　Dà chéngshì de jiāotōng zhēn máfan a
我 说："大 城 市 的 交 通 真 麻 烦 啊！"

司机 说："对 啊！车 开 得 慢，我们 的 客人 就 少 了，还 浪费 时间。生意 真 难 做！"

在 路上，他 不断 地 说 着 各种 社会 问题，说 他 要 养家 有 多么 困难。

到 公司 了。我 的 心情 很 差，马上 跳下 了 车。

几 天 后，我 坐上 了 另外 一 辆 出租车。

马路上，汽车 还是 很 多。我 又 说 了 一 句："大 城市 的 交通 真 麻烦 啊！"

司机 笑 了 一下，说："现在 的 交通 情况 比 以前 好 多 了 。 车 虽然 开 得 慢，但是 还 在 走 啊。"

Taxies waiting for passengers

在路上，他跟我说了很多这个城市的事情。原来这个城市一直在变，变得越来越好。

到公司了。我在下车前，笑着对司机说："谢谢，希望下次还能坐上你的车。"

❷ 喝酒与开车

在一个饭店里，一帮朋友正在为老李庆祝。他今天刚刚收到通知，下个月就要升做经理了。

大家一个接一个地请老李喝酒，老李说："我喝醉就不能开车了！"

一个朋友说："怕什么，车开慢一点就行。今天这么高兴，你不喝，就是不给大家面子，看不起大家了！"

另一个朋友说："你一直都很能

喝酒，这样 几 杯 算 什么。大家 都 为了 你
才 来 吃饭，别 让 大家 不 高兴 啊！"

老李 听 了，觉得 也 有 道理，就 没有 再
坚持，开心 地 接受 朋友 递 过来 的 酒杯。

吃 完 饭，老 李 自己 开车 回家。他 喝
了 很 多 酒，路 都 有点儿 看 不 清楚 了。

一 开始，他 还是 很 小心，车 开 得 很 慢。
后来，发现 路上 的 车 很 少，他 就 放心
了，越 开 越 快，还 开心 地 哼 起 歌 来。

老 李 没 发现 前面 有 一 个 很 急 的 弯。

当 他 想 把 车 停 下来 的 时候，车子 反而
往 前 冲 得 更
快。最后，车子
撞到 马路 旁边
的 大树，翻 了。

躺 在 医院

Tag line in a reminder against drunk driving

里，他 想："要是 坚持 不 喝酒，我 就 不用
在 这里 躺 一 年！"

Translation

❶ Two drivers

I live in a big city. Every morning, many people go to work. Consequently here are also many cars.

One day, I woke up late. I hurriedly got in a taxi, hoping to reach my office faster.

There were many cars on the road, and the taxi was moving slowly.

I said: "The traffic in big cities is such a pain!"

The driver said: "That's right! When traffic is slow, we get fewer customers, and this wastes time as well. Business is really tough!"

Along the way, he kept on talking about various social problems, and how difficult it was for him to support his family.

The taxi reached my office. I was in a bad mood, and immediately got out of the taxi.

A few days later, I got in another taxi.

There were still many cars on the road. Again I said: "The traffic in big cities is such a pain!"

The driver smiled and said: "Traffic is better now than before. The traffic may be slow, but it is still moving."

Along the way, he told me many things about this city. It turns out that the city has been constantly changing, and it is changing for the better.

The taxi reached my office. Before I got out of the taxi, I smiled and said to the driver: "Thank you. I hope to take your taxi again next time."

❷ Drinking and driving

In a hotel, a group of friends was having a celebration for Lao Li. That day he had just received notice that he would be promoted to manager the next month.

One after another, they treated Lao Li to drinks. Lao Li said: "I can't drive if I am drunk!"

One friend said: "What you are afraid of? You just have to drive a little slower. Today is such a happy day. If you don't drink, you are not showing us face, and are looking down on all of us!"

Another friend said: "You have always been a good drinker, so what's a few glasses. Everyone is here because of you, so don't let everyone down!"

Lao Li heard this and thought it made sense. So he did not resist, and happily accepted the drinks from his friends.

After the meal, Lao Li drove himself home. He had drunk a lot, and could not see the road clearly. In the beginning, he was still careful and drove slowly. Later, when he realized that there were few cars on the road, he became relaxed and drove faster and faster, and even started to sing happily.

Lao Li did not notice a sharp bend ahead. He wanted to stop the car, but instead it charged faster ahead. In the end, the car hit a big tree by the road and overturned.

Lying in the hospital, he thought: "If I had insisted on not drinking, I would not need to lie here for a year!"

Safety first

The Chinese people have a habit: when having a meal with family and friends, or socializing with business associates, they like to drink. Many people think that they are good drinkers, and often even drive after drinking. This has led to many accidents that should not have happened in the first place.

Now, in order to tackle the drunk driving situation, the Chinese government has increased the penalties. Previously, when people were caught drunk driving, the most severe penalty was only a fine. But now they will be sent to jail. In addition, police checks on the roads are becoming more frequent. After a few drunk drivers were sentenced to jail, people realized that the government really no longer tolerates drunk drivers. At banquets and social engagements, people are gradually taking the initiative to avoid driving after drinking, and not challenge the law anymore.

As the number of private cars continues to soar, the Chinese government is placing greater emphasis on traffic safety. At driving schools, the standards for learning to drive have become more stringent, in order to reduce the number of potential "road killers". Police officers have also stepped up on law enforcement. When the points deducted for traffic violations reach a certain number, the driver's license will be suspended. There are also many warning signs on the road to remind drivers to be mindful of safety while driving.

Today, "safety first" is once again a phrase that everyone revises daily.

Lǚxíng   de   qǐshì
旅行的启示
Inspiring travels

Pre-reading Questions

I. When you go traveling, do you prefer to travel independently, or to join tour groups? Why?

2. What do you hope to gain the most when you travel?

Duìhuà
❶ 对话

Yǒu yī cì   wǒ hé péngyou zǒu zài lùshang   pèngdào yī
有 一 次，我 和 朋友 走 在 路上，碰到 一

duì wàiguó yóukè xiàng wǒmen wènlù
对 外国 游客 向 我们 问路。

Yuánlái tāmen gēn wǒmen qù xiāngtóng de dìfang wǒmen
原来 他们 跟 我们 去 相同 的 地方，我们

juédìng yīqǐ zǒu
决定 一起 走。

Wǒ wèn tāmen   Nǐmen lái Zhōngguó duō cháng shíjiān
我 问 他们："你们 来 中国 多 长 时间

le
了？"

他们 回答：“一年 了。”

我 说：“一年？你们 不用 工作 吗？”

他们 笑 了，说：“我们 现在 也 在 工作 啊！我们 希望 把 上帝 的 爱 带到 世界 每 一 个 地方。当 人们 遇到 困难，我们 就 去 帮助 他们。中国 也 有 需要 我们 帮助 的 人 啊！”

我 很 奇怪，问：“你们 难道 不用 赚钱 来 照顾 家庭 吗？”

男 游客 说：“她 是 我 的 太太，我们 没有 孩子。从前 的 工作 是 很 能 赚钱 的，但 我们 希望 能 帮助 更 多 的 人。这样 的 生活，比 每 天 只 想 着 怎样 赚钱 更 重要。”

我 和 朋友 感动 了。为了 理想，他们 可以 不 要 高 的 工资，选择 一 种 简单 而 快乐 的 生活。

Wǒmen gāi xiǎngxiang zěnyàng
我们 该 想想，怎样
de shēnghuó cái néng ràng zìjǐ
的 生活 才 能 让 自己
gèng kuàilè Gèzhǒng-gèyàng de
更 快乐？ 各种各样 的
xiǎngshòu háishi chōngmǎn kuàilè
享受， 还是 充满 快乐
de xīn
的 心？

A travel agency with its entrance full of travel advertisements

Lǚxíng de yìyì
❷ 旅行 的 意义

Yī gè xiàwǔ zài dàxué jiàoshì li tóngxuémen
一个 下午，在 大学 教室 里，同学们
zhèngzài wèi bìyè lǚxíng zhǎnkāi yī chǎng tǎolùn
正在 为 毕业 旅行 展开 一 场 讨论。

Yǒude tóngxué shuō Wǒmen yīnggāi cānjiā lǚxíngtuán
有的 同学 说：“我们 应该 参加 旅行团，
zhèyàng yīlùshang chī zhù wán de wèntí dōu bùyòng kǎolù
这样 一路上 吃、住、玩 的 问题 都 不用 考虑
le duō fāngbiàn ya
了，多 方便 呀！”

Yǒude tóngxué shuō Wǒmen yīnggāi zìjǐ jìhuà
有的 同学 说：“我们 应该 自己 计划
lǚxíng lùxiàn zhǎo lǚguǎn zhèyàng cái néng kàndào gèng duō
旅行 路线，找 旅馆，这样 才 能 看到 更 多
píngcháng kàn bù dào de hǎo fēngjǐng
平常 看 不 到 的 好 风景。”

Zhīchí cānjiā lǚxíngtuán de tóngxué yòu shuō Wǒmen
支持 参加 旅行团 的 同学 又 说：“我们

应该 去 看看 其他 城市，体会 一下 那里 的
人，那里 的 生活 有什么 不同。"

支持 自己 计划 旅行 的 同学 说："我们
应该 去 看看 大自然 美丽 的 风景，看看 城市
里 看 不 到 的 东西。"

同学们 在 两 种 意见 中 争 个 不 停。

快 到 晚上 了，还 没有 结果。

这时候，老师 进来，知道 了 怎么 一回事
后，就 笑 着 问 大家："如果 一 次 旅行
能 让 大家 留下 深刻 印象，以后 能 经常
想起，这 不 是 成功 了 吗？去 什么 地方
真的 很 重要 吗？"

老师 的 话 提醒
了 同学们。到底，
旅行 的 意义 是
什么 呢？

Books on independent traveling

56

Translation

❶ Conversation

Once, I was walking with my friends on the street, when a foreign tourist couple asked us for directions.

It turned out that they were going to the same place we were. So we decided to go together.

I asked them: "How long have you been in China?"

They replied: "One year."

I said: "One year? Don't you need to work?"

They smiled and said: "We are also working right now! We hope to spread God's love everywhere in the world. Whenever anyone encounters any difficulty, we will go help them. Even in China there are people who also need our help!"

I was curious, and asked them: "Don't you need to earn money to take care of your family?"

The male tourist said: "She is my wife, and we have no children. Our previous jobs paid very well, so now we hope to help other people. A life like this is more important than thinking about how to make money everyday."

My friends and I were moved. For the sake of their ideals, the couple were willing to give up their high salaries and choose a simple but happy life.

We should think about it. What kind of life will make us happier? All kinds of pleasures, or a heart filled with happiness?

❷ The meaning of travel

One afternoon, in a university classroom, a group of students were having a discussion about their travel plans after graduation.

Some students said: "We should join a tour group. That way, we won't have to think about what to eat, where to stay or where to go. It will be so convenient!"

Other students said: "We should plan the route and find hotels ourselves. That way, we can get to see more sights that we might not usually get to see."

The students who supported joining tour groups said: "We should go take a look at other cities, and understand the people and experience life there."

The students who supported planning their own trip said: "We should go look at beautiful natural scenery, and see things that can't be found in the cities."

The students argued over the two different views. It was almost night, and they still had yet to reach a conclusion.

At that moment, the teacher came in. After learning what the argument was about, she smiled and asked everyone: "If a trip leaves a deep impression on everyone, an experience that everyone will often recall, then isn't that a successful trip? Is the destination really so important?

The teacher's words reminded the students to consider, what really is the meaning of travel?

Exploring sights on your own

Influenced by foreign travelers, independent travel is becoming more and more popular in China. These young people like to be called "背包客" (*beibaoke*; backpackers) as it shows their independent and free side. They have their own views on traveling, and do not blindly follow convention.

In contrast to tour groups where routes are fixed and, with formulaic hotels and sights prearranged, "backpackers" prefer to plan their own itinerary. They will often use various sources of information to understand the unique characteristics of the destination, then decide on transport routes and the itinerary, and find places to eat and stay based on their own preferences.

They do not like five-star hotels, and prefer to stay at youth hostels or guesthouses with distinctive styles. There they can share travel tips with like-minded friends. They do not like to go to run-of-the-mill restaurants and fast food restaurants for meals. Instead, they prefer to comb the streets looking for the most authentic and honest-to-goodness local tastes.

To discover the real side of a place, experience the local life on a deeper level, understand the true customs and practices, broaden one's horizons and derive joy in the process - that is the meaning of independent travel.

To the locals, the arrival of these "背包客" is something fresh that adds novelty to their everyday life.

Like foreign travelers, China's "backpackers" are also discovering different places in the world on their own two feet.

GAMES FOR FUN

Assume you are organizing an independent traveling trip.

Starting from Hong Kong, travel by train to the historic Chinese cities that appear in the map. Follow the requirements below. How will you plan the route?

Requirements:

1. The train fare costs around 1,500 yuan.
2. Include cities in both the south and the north.

Refer to this website for train ticket prices: http://train.qunar.com/

Bù jiǎng jiǎhuà

不讲假话

To tell the truth

Pre-reading Questions

1. In today's commercial society, how important do you think honesty is? Why?

2. Based on your understanding, are Chinese corporations honest? Can you explain why with some examples?

---

①

Sān nián qián bàba dé le zhòngbìng bù néng zài qù
三 年 前，爸爸 得 了 重病，不 能 再 去

gōngzuò Wèile gěi bàba kànbìng wèile ràng wǒ jìxù
工作。为了 给 爸爸 看病，为了 让 我 继续

dúshū māma měi tiān zǎoshang dōu yào dào shìchǎng qù mài
读书，妈妈 每 天 早上 都 要 到 市场 去 卖

shuǐguǒ
水果。

Jīntiān māma yě bìng le Wǒ qǐng māma ràng wǒ qù
今天，妈妈 也 病 了。我 请 妈妈 让 我 去

mài shuǐguǒ Zhèyàng wǒmen jīntiān cái yǒu qián mǎi cài
卖 水果。这样，我们 今天 才 有 钱 买 菜。

Shēngbìng de bàba hé māma yào chī duō diǎn cái néng hǎo
生病 的 爸爸 和 妈妈，要 吃 多 点 才 能 好

起来。
qǐlái

今天要卖的是葡萄。我们用的袋子上
Jīntiān yào mài de shì pútao Wǒmen yòng de dàizishang

写着每袋 500 克。但是，这个袋子装不
xiě zhe měidài kè Dànshì zhège dàizi zhuāng bu

下 500 克的葡萄，只能装 400 克。
xià kè de pútao zhǐ néng zhuāng kè

我把葡萄装进一个个袋子里。每次
Wǒ bǎ pútao zhuāng jìn yīgègè dàizi li Měi cì

有人来问，我就告诉他们这里只有 400
yǒurén lái wèn wǒ jiù gàosu tāmen zhèlǐ zhǐyǒu

克。
kè

一天过去了，我的生意不好。一袋
Yī tiān guòqù le wǒ de shēngyi bù hǎo Yī dài

葡萄都没卖出去。
pútao dōu méi mài chuqu

我想：爸爸妈妈都病了，我要买点
Wǒ xiǎng Bàba māma dōu bìng le wǒ yào mǎi diǎn

肉回去给他们吃。
ròu huíqu gěi tāmen chī

我来到卖肉
Wǒ láidào mài ròu

的地方，希望能
de dìfang xīwàng néng

用葡萄换点肉
yòng pútao huàn diǎn ròu

回家。卖肉的人
huíjiā Mài ròu de rén

答应了。
dāying le

Fruits for sale in a supermarket

❷ 这时候，饭店的老板看到了我的葡萄，就问："孩子，你这葡萄怎么卖？"

我连忙说："葡萄十二块半500克，这里一袋是400克，刚好十块。"

老板问："这一袋是400克吗？可是上面写的是500克。"

我说："真的，不信你可以称一下。"

在卖肉人那儿称了一下，果然是400克。老板笑了，说："孩子，你果然没说假话。你每天都在这里卖葡萄吗？"

我说："不，妈妈病了，今天我代她来卖水果。妈妈说对客人不能说假话，这样客人才会再来买东西。"

老板点点头，说："孩子，你和你妈妈都做得很好。"他又吃了两颗葡萄，笑了，说："你们的葡萄不错啊！以后我们

fàndiàn de shuǐguǒ jiù
饭店 的 水果，就

zhǎo nǐ mǎi kěyǐ
找 你 买，可以

ma
吗？"

Wǒ liánmáng gāoxìng
我 连忙 高兴

de diǎntóu rúguǒ
地 点头，如果

A stall

néng tiāntiān mài shuǐguǒ gěi fàndiàn tāmen de shēngyi jiù huì
能 天天 卖 水果 给 饭店，她们 的 生意 就 会

hǎo hěn duō le Māma shuō de huà chéngzhēn le
好 很 多 了。妈妈 说 的 话 成真 了！

Huíjiā hòu wǒ bǎ zhè jiàn shì gàosu bàba māma
回家 后，我 把 这 件 事 告诉 爸爸 妈妈，

tāmen yě hěn gāoxìng Jīntiān de wǎnfàn wǒmen chī de
他们 也 很 高兴。今天 的 晚饭，我们 吃 得

zuì kāixīn
最 开心。

Translation

❶   Three years ago, my father fell very ill and could no longer go to work. In order to treat my father's illness, and for me to continue my studies, my mother went to the market every morning to sell fruit.

    One day, my mother was ill too. I asked her to let me sell the fruit. This way we would be able to have money to buy groceries for the day. My father and my mother were ill and needed to eat more to recover.

    That day we were selling grapes. On the bags that we used was written that each bag could hold 500 grams. However, the bag was actually too small to hold 500 grams of grapes, and could only take 400 grams.

I filled the bags with grapes. Every time someone asked, I would tell them that there were only 400 grams in each bag.

The day passed, and my business was bad. Not even one bag of grapes was sold.

I thought: Both my father and my mother are sick. I should buy some meat to bring back for them to eat.

I came to the place selling meat, hoping that I could use the grapes to exchange for some meat. The meat seller agreed.

❷　　At that moment, the boss of a restaurant saw my grapes and asked: "Son, how much are you selling your grapes for?"

I quickly said: "The grapes are selling at 12.50 yuan for 500 grams. This bag contains 400 grams, which makes the price 10 yuan."

The boss asked: "Is this bag 400 grams? But it says 500 grams on the bag."

I said: "It's true. If you don't believe me you can weigh it."

A quick weighing at the meat seller's place showed that it was really 400 grams. The boss smiled and said: "Son, so you are really telling the truth. Do you sell grapes here everyday?"

I said: "No, my mother is sick, so today I am selling fruit on her behalf. My mother said we must not lie to customers. Then customers will come back to buy from us again."

The boss nodded and said: "Son, you and your mother have both done well." He ate two grapes, then smiled and said: "Your grapes are not bad! In the future, our restaurant will buy our fruit from you. Is that all right?"

I quickly nodded happily. If we could sell fruit to the restaurant every day, our business would become much better. My mother's words had come true!

When I got back home, I told my father and mother what happened, and they were very happy. The dinner that day was the happiest one we ever had.

Honesty and profit

When buying things in China, many people will often wonder: Is the quality of the item good? Is the weight accurate? Is the price expensive?

Poisonous milk powder, plasticizers, and illegal cooking oil. After so many incidents involving product quality, even the Chinese people are losing confidence in their own products. As a result, situations like these have emerged. Mothers in China go to Hong Kong or Macau, or even overseas, to buy infant milk powder. Everyone is careful about the beverages they drink. People are eating at restaurants less often, and do not even dare to eat the Sichuan cuisine and hotpot that used to be so popular.

The actions of a few unethical businesses have hurt the profits of all. This is a situation that no one wants to see. After years of a mindless chase for profits, people are starting to question themselves: Is it worth giving up long-term benefits for short-term gains?

The answer is of course no. Consumers will only believe in businesses with integrity, and that trust will endure. Having a loyal group of consumers is the best kind of profit for a business.

Hence, in China, when you are shopping online, the website will ask you to consider the store's credibility and consumer ratings. Regardless of whether you are shopping in a store or a market, or when choosing merchandise, the number of satisfied customers will also help you make your choice. After all, a store with good quality products at competitive prices, and honest practices will attract many customers!

GAMES FOR FUN

There are two people, X and Y. Of the two, X only lies and does not tell the truth; Y only tells the truth and does not lie. However, when they are answering other people's questions, they will only nod or shake their head in response, and will not say a single word.

One day, a person faced a choice between two paths: A and

B. One of them leads to the capital city, while the other leads to a small village. Standing in front of him are X and Y, but he does not know which person is X or Y, and does not know if their "nodding" means a "yes" or a "no".

Now, he must ask only one question in order to determine which road leads to the capital. How should he phrase the question?

Érnǚ   de   xiǎngfǎ
儿女的想法
What the children think

Pre-reading Questions

I. How would you describe your relationship with your parents?

2. What do you think an ideal relationship with one's parents is like?

Zuì   hǎo   de   cài
❶ 最 好 的 菜

Yīnwèi   māma   hěn   zǎo   jiù   sǐ   le   suǒyǐ   bàba   dài
因为 妈妈 很 早 就 死 了，所以 爸爸 带

zhe   nǚ'ér   liǎng   gè   rén   shēnghuó
着 女儿，两 个 人 生活。

Yǒu   yī   tiān   bàba   xiàbān   huíjiā   hěn   lèi
有 一 天，爸爸 下班 回家，很 累。

Tā   dǎkāi   le   mén   fāxiàn   jiāli   hěn   luàn   Zhuōzishang
他 打开 了 门，发现 家里 很 乱。桌子上

fàng   zhe   liǎng   pán   hēihēide   dōngxi   nǚ'ér   jiù   shuì   zài
放 着 两 盘 黑黑的 东西，女儿 就 睡 在

shāfāshang
沙发上。

Bàba   hěn   shēngqì   bǎ   nǚ'ér   jiào   qǐlai   dàshēng   wèn
爸爸 很 生气，把 女儿 叫 起来，大声 问

tā
她："为什么把家里弄得这么乱？"

Nǚ'ér dī zhe tóu xiǎoshēng shuō Jīntiān shì nǐ de
女儿低着头，小声说："今天是你的

shēngri Wǒ xiǎng zìjǐ zuò yī dùn fàn gěi nǐ chī Zhèxiē
生日。我想自己做一顿饭给你吃。这些

cài dōu shì māma chángcháng zuò gěi nǐ chī de
菜都是妈妈常常做给你吃的。"

Bàba tīng le méiyǒu shuōhuà Tā jìngjìngde chī zhe
爸爸听了，没有说话。他静静地吃着

zhuōzishang de cài
桌子上的菜。

Nǚ'ér wèn tā Bàba cài hǎochī ma
女儿问他："爸爸，菜好吃吗？"

Bàba xiào le
爸爸笑了，

shuō Zhè shì wǒ
说："这是我

chī guo de zuì hǎo de
吃过的最好的

cài
菜！"

Home-cooked food of the Chinese people

Bàba nín fàngxīn
❷ 爸爸，您放心

Tā cóngxiǎo jiù zài nóngcūn zhǎngdà Tā bàba de tuǐ
他从小就在农村长大。他爸爸的腿

yǒu bìng bù néng zǒulù
有病，不能走路。

Tā kǎo shàng dàxué bàba hěn gāoxìng Tā shuō
他考上大学，爸爸很高兴。他说：

"爸爸，您放心，读完书，我就有钱治好您的腿，让您过好的生活。"

四年后，他读完书，找到了一份在工厂修机器的工作。他每天都认真地工作。

第一年春节回家，爸爸看到他黑黑的手指，不放心地说："孩子，你找的工作一定很脏很累。我的腿不要治了，你换一份工作吧！"

他笑了笑，对爸爸说："您放心吧，我的工作挺好，一点都不累。"

第二年春节回家，爸爸看到他瘦了，更加不放心，说："孩子，那工作别干了！"

他说："爸爸，您放心，我现在工作得很开心！"

Dì-sān nián Chūn Jié tā zhōngyú bǎ bàba jiēdào tā
第 三 年 春 节 ， 他 终 于 把 爸 爸 接 到 他

gōngzuò de chéngshì Bàba dào dà yīyuàn zhì hǎo le tuǐ
工 作 的 城 市 。 爸 爸 到 大 医 院 治 好 了 腿 ，

zhù zài tā zū de xīn fángzi li
住 在 他 租 的 新 房 子 里 。

Zǒujìn fángzi de
走 进 房 子 的

yī kè bàba xiào
一 刻 ， 爸 爸 笑

le tā yě xiào le
了 ， 他 也 笑 了 。

A factory

Translation

❶ The best dish

Ever since the mother passed away many years ago, the father and the daughter had lived together.

One day, the father got home from work and was tired.

He opened the door and found that the house was very messy. On the table were two plates of blackish stuff, and the daughter was asleep on the sofa.

The father was angry. He woke the daughter up and asked her in a loud voice: "Why did you make the house so messy?"

The daughter lowered her head and said softly: "Today is your birthday. I wanted to cook a meal for you. These dishes are what mother used to make for you."

Upon hearing this, the father did not say anything. He quietly ate the food on the table.

The daughter asked: "Father, are the dishes okay?"

The father smiled and said: "These are the best dishes I have ever eaten!"

❷ Father, don't worry

A young man grew up in the countryside. His father had bad legs and was unable to walk.

When the young man made it to university, his father was very happy. He said: "Father, don't worry. When I finish my studies, I will have money to treat your legs, so you will have a good life."

Four years later, he finished his studies, and found a job repairing machines in a factory. He worked hard every day.

The first year, when he returned home for the Spring Festival, his father saw his blackened fingers, and said worriedly: "Son, your job must be dirty and tiring. My legs do not need to be treated. Why don't you change your job!"

The young man smiled and said to his father: "Don't worry, my job is quite good, and is not tiring at all."

The second year, when he returned home for the Spring Festival, his father saw he had lost weight, and was even more worried. He said: "Son, why don't you quit your job!"

He said: "Father, don't worry, I am happy in my job!"

The third year, during the Spring Festival, the young man brought his father to the city where he worked. His father had his legs treated at a big hospital, and lived in the new place that his son had rented.

When they entered the house, his father smiled. So did he.

The helpless young people who live off their parents

In China, there is a group of young people who are now dubbed啃老族 (*kenlaozu*; "those who live off the old").

The term 啃老 (*kenlao*) refers to those who are not only unable to support their parents, but are also dependent on their parents or elders in the family for financial support and connections.

You might think this is strange. These young people have already joined the workforce, so why can't they be self-reliant and take charge of their own lives?

Typically, for most young people in China, if their workplace and family are in the same city, they will continue to live with their parents before they get married. Some of them do not earn enough to live independently, and are unable to pay their parents for their own meals, much less support their parents. Moreover, Chinese people usually want to purchase a new place before getting married. In China, housing prices are now getting higher and higher. For these young people, the savings accumulated from just a few years of work are not enough to pay the expensive housing loans. That is why they still need to depend on their parents' savings, which have accumulated over decades, to help them fulfill their wish of getting married and setting up a family.

Being a 啃老 (*kenlao*) is actually a choice made out of helplessness in the face of societal realities. In the hearts of these young people, filial piety is a deep-rooted notion. They do not want to rely on their parents, and want to earn more money to support their parents. But not everyone is able to find a good job. So they can only depend on their parents for the time being while they continue to work hard. They deeply hope that one day they will be able to support their parents in living a good life together with them.

Liǎng zhǒng   shēnghuó

两种生活

Two different lifestyles

Pre-reading Questions

I. What is your dream life like? This could be misinterpreted as something about dreams, so perhaps ideal life is better?

2. Do you have some idea about what life is like in big Chinese cities for people from different walks of life?

---

❶
Tāmen   cóng   nóngcūn   láidào   chéngshì   gōngzuò   Nánren   zài
他们 从 农村 来到 城市 工作。男人 在

gōngchǎng   dāng   gōngrén   nǚren   zài   biéren   jiāli   dǎgōng
工厂 当 工人，女人 在 别人 家里 打工。

Tāmen   měi   gè   yuè   de   shōurù   bù   duō   zhǐyǒu   liǎngqiān   duō   yuán
他们 每 个 月 的 收入 不 多，只有 两千 多 元。

Tāmen   zhù   zài   xiǎoxiǎo   de   fángzi . li   méiyǒu   diànshì
他们 住 在 小小 的 房子 里，没有 电视，

méiyǒu   jìsuànjī
没有 计算机。

Měi   tiān   chī   wán   fàn   méiyǒu   qítā   huódòng   zhǐnéng   dào
每 天 吃 完 饭，没有 其它 活动，只能 到

lí   jiā   bù   yuǎn   de   xiǎo   gōngyuán   zǒu   yi   zǒu
离 家 不 远 的 小 公园 走 一 走。

他们 总是 拉着 手，一边 走，一边 说着
生活 中 发生 的 事情。

为了 一些 小 事，他们 有时候 会 不断
讨论，有时候 又 会 小 声 说，大 声 笑。

❷ 她 的 先生 是 商人，他 给 她 很 多 钱，
很 少 回家。

她 住 在 漂亮 的 大 房子 里，家里 什么
都 有。她 家 放 衣服 的 房间，比 一般 人 的
房子 还要 大。

她 不用 工作，事情 都 是 花 钱 请 人
回来 做 的。

每 天 吃 完 饭，她 可以 做 很 多 事情：
看 电视，听 音乐，上网，看书，在 花园 走
一 走。如果 她 愿意，还 可以 跟 朋友们 一起
喝酒，唱歌，跳舞。

她 想 干 什么 就 干 什么。

可是，她还是喜欢一个人吃饭，然后
到离家不远的小公园去走一走。

A park for people to relax

❸ 有一天，男人和女人吃完饭，又到
小公园去了。

她吃过晚饭，也去了小公园。

走得累了，男人和女人就在长椅上
坐下来。这时，她就坐在旁边的一张
椅子上。

男人 对 女人 说："等 我 以后 有 钱 了，就 买 一 间 大 房子，还要 买 电视机，你 就 可以 天天 看 喜欢 的 电视 节目 了。"

女人 说："如果 你 有 钱 了，也许 就 没有 时间 和 我 一起 到 公园 来 了。"

男人 说："不 去 公园，我 就 和 你 一起 看 电视 好 了。"

女人 开心 地 笑 了。

她 听到 他们 的 话，心里 想："钱 再 多 有 什么 用 呢？两 个 人 一起 看 电视，去 公园，才是 最 开心 的 啊！"

Translation

❶ A couple from the countryside came to work in the city. The man was a worker in a factory, while the woman was a domestic worker. Their monthly income was not much, only two thousand plus yuan.

They stayed in a small place with no television set and no computer.

Every day after they had their meal, there was nothing else to do, and so they would go to a small park near their home to take a walk.

They always walked hand in hand, and as they walked they would talk about what happened in their everyday life.

They would sometimes discuss trivial matters at length. Sometimes they would speak softly, or laugh loudly.

❷ A lady's husband was a businessman. He gave her a lot of money, but he was seldom at home.

She lived in a beautiful big house that had everything. The room where she kept her clothes was bigger than the house of an average person.

She did not need to work, as people were paid to do things for her.

Every day after meals, she could do many things: Watch television, listen to music, surf the Internet, read books, take a walk in the garden. If she wanted, she could also drink with her friends, or go singing or dancing.

She could do whatever she wanted.

However, the lady still liked to eat alone, and then go to a small park near her home to take a walk.

❸ One day, the man and the woman had finished their meal, and they went to the small park again.

The lady had her dinner, and also went to the small park.

When they were tired from walking, the man and the woman sat down on a long bench. The lady happened to be sitting on the same bench next to them.

The man said to the woman: "When I have the money, I will buy a big house, and a television as well. Every day you can watch all the television programs that you like."

The woman said: "If you have the money, you might not have time to come to the park with me."

The man said: "Then we will not go to the park. I will watch television with you."

The woman smiled happily.

The lady heard their conversation, and thought to herself: "What is the use of having so much money? Watching television and going to the park together is truly the happiest thing!"

The kind of life that you want

What kind of life do you want?

If you were to ask this question to Chinese people, most of them will reply: To have a house and a car, have no worries in life, and a happy family.

You might find it strange that the Chinese people include having a house and a car in their standard of an ideal life. This could have something to do with the traditional Chinese idea of settling down and living a stable life. The Chinese people like to own their own property, so it is only after they have bought their house that they feel that it is really their own home. As for cars, Chinese people view this goal as a symbol of improvement in their quality of life. Hence, the owning of one or more cars has become one of their pursuits for a higher quality of life.

While pursuing material life, the Chinese people also hope to have a happy family. This is not easy. In the allotment of time, work and family are always two conflicting sides. People are often trying hard to achieve a balance between work, income and family life. They want to have a successful career and a higher income, and at the same time they want to be able to take care of their family and ensure that their family lives happily. And because it is so difficult to balance both, this has become an ideal kind of life.

Nowadays, many people, especially young people, will have even more hopes for their ideal life, such as: To have a healthy body, to have the time and money to travel every year, to be able to constantly upgrade their abilities, to have energy to spare to help people in need.

In the future, if you were to ask the same question, perhaps you might get an answer where both spiritual life and and material life are equally important.

Fùmǔ   de   gǎnqíng
父母的感情
Relationship with parents

Pre-reading Questions

1. Are your parents strict with you? How do you view their demands on you?

2. What do you most wish to do together with your parents? Why?

Bàba   yě   huì yòng diànnǎo
❶ 爸爸 也 会 用 电脑

Xiǎo Míng fāxiàn   bàba   zuìjìn   biàn   le
小 明 发现 爸爸 最近 变 了。

Zài Xiǎo Míng qù Měiguó dú dàxué zhīqián   bàba   yīdiǎn
在 小 明 去 美国 读 大学 之前，爸爸 一点

dōu bù xǐhuan diànnǎo
都 不 喜欢 电脑。

Xiǎo Míng shuō   Bàba   wǒ zài Měiguó yào mǎi yī tái
小 明 说：“爸爸，我 在 美国 要 买 一 台

diànnǎo   Bàba   shuō   Nǐ zǒngshì xiǎng zhe wán diànnǎo
电脑。”爸爸 说：“你 总是 想 着 玩 电脑，

jiù méiyǒu shíjiān dúshū   le   bù néng mǎi
就 没有 时间 读书 了，不 能 买。”

小明又说："爸爸，现在人人都会用电脑了，怎么你不去学呢？"爸爸说："我不需要电脑。所有事情我记得很清楚，要电脑有什么用？"

现在，爸爸打电话给小明，说："下一次，我们用电脑联系吧！"

小明很奇怪：爸爸什么时候买电脑了？爸爸又怎么学会用电脑的呢？

这天，小明终于和爸爸在电脑里"见面"。

小明急着问："爸爸！你怎么学会电脑的？谁给你买的电脑？你学电脑用了多长时间？"

爸爸笑着说："别人对我说，用电脑和你见面，又便宜又快，还很容易就找到你。所以我就赶紧买了一台，花了两个星期就学会了!你爸爸聪明吗?"

小明听完,想到平常节省的爸爸去

买电脑,然后每天一点一点学用电脑的

样子,心都痛了。不过,他还是笑着说:

"我爸爸是最聪明的!以后我会常用

电脑去找你!"

❷ 裤子太短了

女儿收到一家大公司的通知,要参加

考试,才可以得到工作的机会。

她准备了一条新裤子,打算在考试

那天穿。

考试的前一天,女儿发现裤子长了

一点,就请妈妈帮忙改一下。奶奶在

旁边也听到了。

晚饭之后,女儿去为考试做准备,

māma qù xǐ wǎn le
妈妈 去 洗 碗 了。

Nǎinai kàndào dàjiā dōu zài máng xiǎng Ràng wǒ
奶奶 看到 大家 都 在 忙，想："让 我

lái bāngmáng gǎi kùzi ba
来 帮忙 改 裤子 吧。"

Tā bǎ kùzi gǎi duǎn le yīdiǎn mǎnyì de huí le
她 把 裤子 改 短 了 一点，满意 地 回 了

zìjǐ de fángjiān
自己 的 房间。

Māma xǐ le wǎn jìqi nǚ'ér de huà jiù náqi
妈妈 洗 了 碗，记起 女儿 的 话，就 拿起

gōngjù bǎ kùzi gǎi duǎn le yīdiǎn Gǎi hǎo zhīhòu
工具，把 裤子 改 短 了 一点。改 好 之后，

māma xiǎng Míngtiān nǚ'ér chuānshàng yīdìng hěn hǎokàn
妈妈 想："明天 女儿 穿上 一定 很 好看！"

Dì-èr tiān nǚ'ér qǐchuáng hòu chuānshàng kùzi dà
第二 天，女儿 起床 后，穿上 裤子，大

jiào qilai Māma kùzi tài duǎn le
叫 起来："妈妈，裤子 太 短 了！"

Māma hé nǎinai yīqǐ pǎo chulai cái zhīdao yuánlái
妈妈 和 奶奶 一起 跑 出来，才 知道 原来

tāmen dōu gǎi guo kùzi
她们 都 改 过 裤子。

Nǎinai yǒu diǎn hàipà shuō Zěnmebàn ne Dōu shì
奶奶 有 点 害怕，说："怎么 办 呢？都 是

nǎinai bù hǎo bù gāi zìjǐ qù gǎi
奶奶 不 好，不 该 自己 去 改。"

Zhèshíhou nǚ'ér xiào zhe shuō Nǎinai māma
这时候，女儿 笑 着 说："奶奶，妈妈，

xièxie nǐmen Zhè tiáo kùzi duǎn le méi guānxi yǐhòu
谢谢 你们！这 条 裤子 短 了 没 关系，以后

<ruby>还<rt>hái</rt></ruby> <ruby>可<rt>kěyǐ</rt></ruby> <ruby>以<rt></rt></ruby> <ruby>穿<rt>chuān</rt></ruby> ， <ruby>今<rt>jīntiān</rt></ruby> <ruby>天<rt></rt></ruby> <ruby>我<rt>wǒ</rt></ruby> <ruby>可<rt>kěyǐ</rt></ruby> <ruby>以<rt></rt></ruby> <ruby>穿<rt>chuān</rt></ruby> <ruby>别<rt>biéde</rt></ruby> <ruby>的<rt></rt></ruby> <ruby>裤<rt>kùzi</rt></ruby> <ruby>子<rt></rt></ruby> ！ <ruby>有<rt>Yǒu</rt></ruby>
<ruby>你<rt>nǐmen</rt></ruby> <ruby>们<rt></rt></ruby> <ruby>的<rt>de</rt></ruby> <ruby>关<rt>guānxīn</rt></ruby> <ruby>心<rt></rt></ruby> ， <ruby>我<rt>wǒ</rt></ruby> <ruby>今<rt>jīntiān</rt></ruby> <ruby>天<rt></rt></ruby> <ruby>一<rt>yīdìng</rt></ruby> <ruby>定<rt></rt></ruby> <ruby>能<rt>néng</rt></ruby> <ruby>成<rt>chénggōng</rt></ruby> <ruby>功<rt></rt></ruby> ！ ”

A shop that alters clothes

Translation

❶ Father also knows how to use the computer

Xiao Ming realized that his father had changed recently.

Before Xiao Ming went to university in America, his father did not like computers at all.

Xiao Ming had said: "Father, I want to buy a computer in America." His father replied: "You will always be thinking of playing on the computer, and then you will have no time to study. No, you cannot buy one."

Xiao Ming then said: "Father, everybody now knows how to use a computer. Why don't you learn how?" His father said: "I don't need a computer. I remember everything clearly. What do I need a computer for?"

Now, his father called Xiao Ming and said: "Next time, we'll contact each other using the computer!"

Xiao Ming thought this was strange: When did his father buy a computer? How did his father learn to use a computer?

Then one day, Xiao Ming finally "met" his father on the computer.

Xiao Ming hurriedly asked: "Father! How did you learn to use the computer? Who bought you the computer? How long did it take you to learn how to use the computer?"

Father smiled and said: "Other people told me that using the computer to contact you would be cheap and fast, and I would be able to find you easily. So I quickly bought one, and learned how to use it in two weeks! Isn't your father clever?"

After hearing this, Xiao Ming thought about how his usually thrifty father went to buy a computer, and how he learned to use it bit by bit every day, just so he could be in contact with his son, and it made his heart ache. However, he still smiled and said: "My father is the smartest! In future, I will often expect to find you on the computer!"

❷ The pants are too short

A young woman received notice from a big company that she had to take a test before she could get a job opportunity.

She prepared a new pair of pants, and planned to wear them on the day of the test.

The day before the test, the woman realized that the pants were a little too long, and asked her mother to help alter them. Her grandmother was nearby and heard it as well.

After dinner, the woman went to prepare for her test, and her mother went to wash the dishes.

The grandmother saw that everyone was busy, and thought: "Let me help to alter the pants."

She made the pants a little shorter, and returned to her room satisfied.

After washing the dishes, the mother remembered what her daughter said, and picked up her tools and made the pants a little shorter. When she was done with the alteration, the mother thought: "Tomorrow my daughter will look good in these!"

The next day, the young woman got up, put on the pants, and cried out: "Mother, the pants are too short!"

Her mother and grandmother both came running, and only then did they realize that both of them had altered the pants.

Grandmother panicked and said: "What should we do? It's all grandma's fault, I should not have altered them…"

But the young woman smiled and said: "Grandmother, mother, thank you both! It doesn't matter that this pair of pants is short. I can still wear them in the future. Today I can wear another pair of pants! With your concern, I will definitely succeed today!"

So great the parents' love for their children

There is an old saying in China that goes: "*keliantianxiafumuxin*" (可怜天下父母心). It means that the wholehearted devotion and ardent expectations that all parents have for their children is touching.

This phrase can be used to describe parents in China for the past few thousand years. Today, due to China's unique family planning policy, many families can only raise one child. Hence parents are even more devoted to their children.

Even before the child is born, young parents are already thinking of ways to give the child more nutrition, and engaging in prenatal education, in the hope that the child will be more intelligent;

After the child is born, the parents are eager to give him the best. As much as their finances allow, their child will always get the best of everything, be it food or other things.

The child's education is the most important part. To get their child into good schools, parents will not hesitate to spend tens or even hundreds of thousands of yuan. To give their child an edge in their studies, parents scramble to sign them up for tuition classes that cost more than ten thousand yuan per semester.

Even when their children are already working or getting married, as long as there is a need, most parents continue to provide support to their children. For example, parents may help to finance their children's wedding preparations, or buy them a place to stay.

Because of this, children in China tend to be more reliant on their parents than children in other countries. But it is also because of this that children in China have closer relations with their parents, and place more importance on their family.

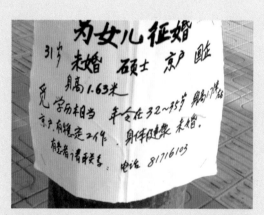

An advertisement by parents seeking a marriage partner for their daughter

GAMES FOR FUN

In China, on the birthdays of their parents or other elder members of the family, the children will often prepare "长寿面"(*changshoumian*; longevity noodles) for them. Try making some for your parents!

1. Ingredients: 1 cup of flour (measuring cup used for cooking rice), 1 egg, lean pork, 2 green onions.
2. Place the flour into a bowl and mix the egg into the flour. Add a

little salt (salt will make the noodles more chewy). Use your hands to knead the mixture into a smooth dough.

3. Use a moist cloth to cover the dough, and let the moisture from the cloth seep evenly into the dough.

4. Cut the meat into thin strips. Marinate it with ginger strips, cooking wine and a little oil.

5. Sprinkle flour on your countertop. Roll the dough into a flat and round piece that is 1 mm thick.

6. Use a knife to make circular cuts that are 1 cm wide. Start from the outer edge of the dough and cut towards the center. If you lift the noodle from the outer edge, you will get one long noodle.

7. Boil water in a pot. Add a little salt and put in the noodles. Add cold water 3 times and the noodles will be cooked.

8. Rinse the cooked noodles in cold water. Place the noodles in the pork soup that is prepared separately. Sprinkle chopped green onions on top. Your lovingly prepared bowl of longevity noodles is now ready.

Longevity noodles

Glossary

Common Words and Phrases			GCS Rank	Page
shēng yi	生意	business	1	*3*
xiǎo chī	小吃	snack	2	*2*
yǐn liào	饮料	beverage	2	*4*
jīng yíng	经营	operate	1	*3*
xuǎn zé	选择	choose	2	*4*
gōng fu	功夫	efforts	1	*5*
cā	擦	polish	2	*9*
běn dì	本地	local	2	*9*
shū shu	叔叔	uncle	2	*10*
zhuàn	赚	earn	2	*10*
tuán tǐ	团体	organization	1	*11*
zhěng zhěng	整整	whole	1	*10*
wǎng luò	网络	internet	1	*10*
rèn zhēn	认真	seriously	1	*10*
jiā xiāng	家乡	hometown	1	*10*
dì tiě zhàn	地铁站	subway station	1	*11*
zháo jí	着急	worry	1	*11*
gǎn jǐn	赶紧	hurry up	1	*12*
yì wài	意外	accident	1	*13*
ān jìng	安静	quite	1	*13*
zhuā zhu	抓住	grasp	1	*12*
zhù yì	注意	pay attention to	1	*11*
shòu huò yuán	售货员	salesman	2	*16*
rè qíng	热情	enthusiasm	1	*2*

GCS: HanBan / Confucius Institute Headquaters, The Graded Chinese Syllables, Characters and Words for the Application of Teaching Chinese to the Speakers of Other Languages, 2010.

yōu huì	优惠	premium	2	18
pián yi	便宜	cheap	1	16
chāo shì	超市	supermarket	1	18
kǎo shì	考试	examination	1	25
kǎo yàn	考验	test	1	25
tí mù	题目	topic	2	25
jǐn zhāng	紧张	nervous	1	25
fù zé	负责	responsible for	1	25
lǎo bǎn	老板	boss	1	23
jiā bān	加班	work overtime	2	23
nán tí	难题	difficult problem	2	24
piào liang	漂亮	pretty	1	30
jīng lì	经历	come through	1	31
biàn huà	变化	change	1	31
jié hūn	结婚	marriage	1	31
jiè zhi	戒指	ring	3	31
hūn lǐ	婚礼	wedding	3	31
zuàn shí	钻石	diamond	3	32
gǎn qíng	感情	emotions	1	31
qū bié	区别	difference	1	32
xiào liǎn	笑脸	smiling face	2	34
bān jiā	搬家	move house	2	34
xiǎo tōu	小偷	thief	2	39
fū fù	夫妇	couple	2	41
gǎn mào	感冒	cold	2	41
dēng guāng	灯光	lamplight	2	41

shōu shi	收拾	tidy	2	42
shuì jiào	睡觉	sleep	1	42
sī jī	司机	driver	1	46
chū zū chē	出租车	taxi	1	46
má fan	麻烦	trouble	1	47
miàn zi	面子	reputation; face	2	48
zuì	醉	drunk	2	48
jiān chí	坚持	insist	1	4
qīng chu	清楚	clear	1	39
zhuàng	撞	crash	2	50
tǎng	躺	lay	2	50
gōng zī	工资	wage	1	24
gǎn dòng	感动	be moved	1	10
zhuàn qián	赚钱	make money	2	24
zhào gù	照顾	take care	1	54
shēn kè	深刻	deep	1	56
tí xǐng	提醒	remind	2	56
bì yè	毕业	graduate	2	55
kǎo lǜ	考虑	consider	1	55
pú tao	葡萄	grape	2	61
lián máng	连忙	at once	1	62
cōng ming	聪明	clever	2	81
jié shěng	节省	frugal	2	81
kù zi	裤子	pants	2	81